Shaggy Dog's HALLOWEEN

written and illustrated by Donald Charles

CHILDRENS PRESS ™

CHICAGO

For Fran

Library of Congress Cataloging in Publication Data

Charles, Donald.
  Shaggy Dog's Halloween.

  Includes index.
  Summary: Shaggy Dog's invitation to a Halloween
party inspires a number of ideas for a costume, but
Calico Cat helps him make the final decision.
  [1. Halloween—Fiction. 2. Dogs—Fiction. 3. Cats—
Fiction] I. Title.
PZ7.C374Sf 1984   [E]   84-5901
ISBN 0-516-03575-4

Shaggy Dog's
HALLOWEEN

Shaggy Dog is
invited to a
Halloween party.

Shaggy Dog
will wear
a costume.

Maybe he will
be a monster.

Maybe he will
be a bat.

He might be
a skeleton,

or wear a
cowboy hat.

He might wear
a clown suit.

He could paint
his face.

Maybe he will
be a witch,

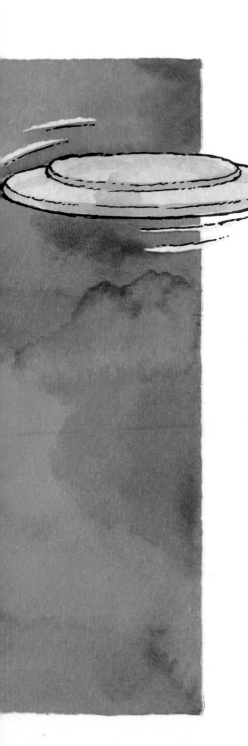

or a thing
from outer space.

His friend,
Calico Cat,
has an idea.

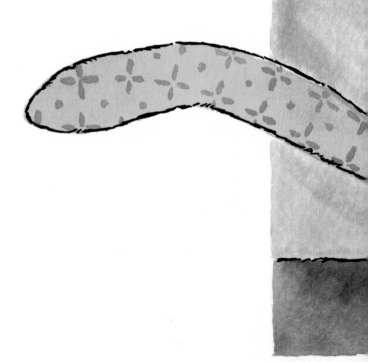

They are making
masks from
paper bags.

Now they're ready
for the party.

Shaggy Dog can make a mask. Can you?

YOU NEED:

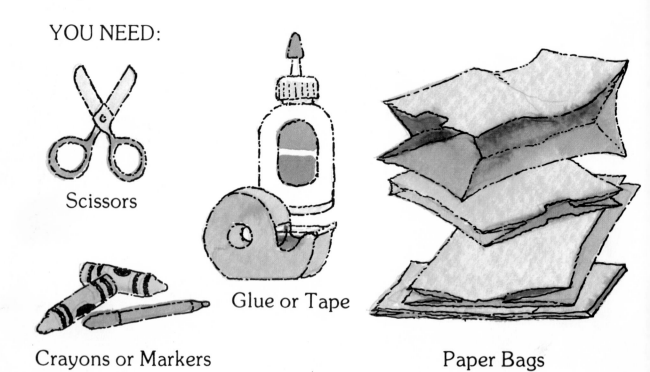

Scissors

Glue or Tape

Crayons or Markers

Paper Bags

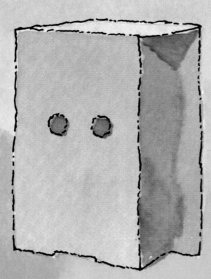

1. Cut or tear eye holes.

2. Paste on pieces of paper for ears, nose, or hair.

3. Draw mouth and color.

ABOUT THE AUTHOR/ARTIST

Donald Charles started his long career as an artist and author more than twenty-five years ago after attending the University of California and the Art League School of California. He began by writing and illustrating feature articles for the San Francisco Chronicle, and also sold cartoons and ideas to The New Yorker and Cosmopolitan magazines. Since then he has been, at various times, a longshoreman, ranch hand, truck driver, and editor of a weekly newspaper, all enriching experiences for a writer and artist. Ultimately he became creative director for an advertising agency, a post which he resigned several years ago to devote himself full-time to book illustration and writing. Mr. Charles has received frequent awards from graphic societies, and his work has appeared in numerous textbooks and periodicals.